Polly's Running Away Book

Bloomsbury Publishing, London, Berlin, New York and Sydney

First published in Great Britain in August 2000 by Bloomsbury Publishing Plc
50 Bedford Square, London, WC1B 3DP

This paperback edition published in March 2012

A CIP catalogue record for this book is available from the British Library

ISBN 978 1 4088 2515 0

MIX
Paper from
responsible sources
FSC   www.fsc.org   FSC® C018072

Typeset by Hewer Text UK Ltd, Edinburgh
Printed in Great Britain by Clays Ltd, St Ives Plc, Bungay, Suffolk

1 3 5 7 9 10 8 6 4 2

www.bloomsbury.com

Polly's Running Away Book

Written by Frances Thomas

Illustrated by Sally Gardner

BLOOMSBURY

LONDON BERLIN NEW YORK SYDNEY

Really really stupid.

WEDNESDAY

Things I like about my life:
NOTHING.

Things I hate about my
life: EVERYTHING.

THURSDAY

Anyway, I am Running
Away soon. This is my
Running Away Book.

I am saving up. So far I
have got 96p and one
Double Decker.

Horace has run away too.

- away - - - - - - - - -

He is our hamster. He has been missing two days.

Dad says he will come back but how does he know?

They pretend they know everything but they don't.

They say things just to shut you up but I am NOT SILLY.

I said to Mum, it is not fair, Kelly isn't my best friend any more. Yesterday she was my best friend but today she said Lisa was going to be her best friend and anyway she had a secret. I said that it was not

Horace running

fair of people to be your
best friend one day and then
change their minds. It is silly
of her to keep having secrets.
All Mum said was, not now
darling.

She should listen to me
when I am telling her things.

FRIDAY
Miss Price says you
can't just hate something.
You have to say why.

I hate her. She is a
DER-BRAIN.

Mum says I am going
through a STROPPY FAZE.

I hate her. She is always

8

going on at me to:

Tidy Your Clothes

Don't Shout at Mopsy

Wear Skirts

Eat Your BROCERLY.

Dad says, what happened

to my dear little Princess?

He is IRRITATING me.

When I was little I used
to want to be a Princess
but now I'm not bothered.

Anyway, Mopsy is
stupid because:

She likes Waybuloo

She has a pink handbag

She is three

She talks to ants

She doesn't like:

mushrooms, tomatoes,
pasta, cheese, anything
with garlic and lumpy bits.

I only don't like
BROCERLY.

I don't think I have
spelt it right. Miss Price
says 'ALWAYS look it up'

but why should I look it
up when I don't even like
it?

Mum is always tired,
She says it will be better
when the new baby comes.

WHO WANTS A NEW
BABY ANYWAY –
    NOT ME!!!

I think it is unfair of her
to say the NEW baby all the
time. She should think
about her proper children
a bit more.

Horace has been away
three days
    I still have 96p.
    I have one Double
Decker and a Nutella
sandwich from tea.

MONDAY
Kelly's secret is that she is
going to DISNEYLAND! She
is going on and on about
it. They are going in the
holidays. They are going

on the train to France. She says she won't bring me a present. She will bring Lisa a present.

I don't care. Disneyland is smelly.

Kelly isn't my best friend. She used to be my best friend.

Some people always go on and on about things.

We are starting the Tudors. They lived in wooden houses and threw their poo out of the windows. I said, I think the Tudors were smelly. Miss Price said they probably

were, but then people were smelly in olden days.

Darren Biggs said Some People are still smelly.

Yes, like Darren Biggs. I don't like him anyway.

Alex will probably be my best friend now.

Miss Price is called Julia. She is twenty-seven. Her boyfriend is Nigel. He is In Banking. She sends him texts in the classroom. She thinks we don't know.

She is not getting married yet but she might next year. She will get married in a REGISTRAR

OFFICE. She doesn't
want bridesmaids.

She should not wear
Pink. It matches her
nose. She should
wear blue or green.
And not dangly
earrings.

17

Mrs Muldoon

Mrs Kirby

Mrs Shah

Mr Jarvis

Mrs Muldoon is our Headmistress. She is nice sometimes, except when she is being nasty.

Last year we were in Mrs Kirby's class. She was brilliant. Next year it will probably be Mr Jarvis or Mrs Shah. I hope Mrs Shah.

It's not fair. I said to Dad, can we go to Disneyland because Kelly's going to Disneyland and he said, ooh, Polly. He said, I don't think so, pet, not this year anyway because of the new baby and not having lots of money.

I said, what will be our
holiday then this year, and
he said, ooh, Polly again.
He said, maybe this year
we might not have a
holiday! It is SO not fair.

Horace – 6 days
Running Away Money – 96p
2 Double Deckers
1 Nutella sandwich

TUESDAY
I found a 20p in the street.
Dad said it wasn't
enough for stealing, so it
was all right. I said, when
did it start being stealing? He
said, well, perhaps £5.

I said would £1 be? He didn't know.

I said would 50p be? He said, oh Poll, stop asking questions.

In Diary we talked about holidays. Kelly went on and on about Guess What. Luke is going to Italy and Trixie is going to Spain. Oliver said they went to Italy last year and he said they had

dead snake

a dead snake in their
swimming pool. In Italy they
call Mickey Mouse Topolino.
That is really dumb.

John said he hopes they go
to Center Parcs.

We went to Center Parcs
last year. It was brilliant. We
rode our bikes all the time
and I made friends with a
girl called Lee. She had three
Barbie dolls and a Barbie
palace. Plus she had two
teddies and a dog called
Sukie. Not a real dog, a

toy dog. She was nice but she had to take her Barbies everywhere, which was a bit boring.

I don't have a Barbie doll. I did but Mopsy pulled the head off. I don't really mind as she wasn't my best doll anyway.

Then another time we went to France. France is just like England except the people speak very fast in French all the time. You say GLAS for ice cream and POMFREET for chips. MERCY BOCOO — I don't know how you spell it — is thank you very much. You have to be very polite to French people.

I would quite like to go to France again but I would prefer to go to Center Parcs. It is very unfair not having a holiday because of a stupid baby that nobody wants anyway.

Horace – 7 days
Running Away Money – £1.16
2 Double Deckers
1 Nutella sandwich
1 Snickers
bar

Kelly and Lisa kept walking round the playground together. They were pretending to be sisters. They said, 'We're REALLY sisters not PRETEND sisters.'

Alex said, let's be sisters as well but I didn't want to. It is bad enough having a real sister.

Kelly said I was not her best friend and I had never been her best friend because Lisa always always was. That is not true because she used to think Lisa was babyish.

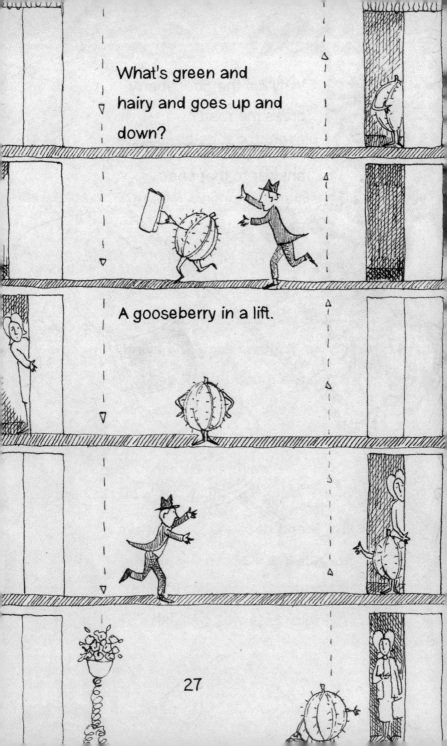

What's green and hairy and goes up and down?

A gooseberry in a lift.

27

Why did the gooseberry
cross the road?
    I can't remember the
answer to that one.

SATURDAY
THINGS I LIKE:
Crispy Duck
Prawn Toast

We went for a Chinese meal today. Mum said it might be the last chance before You-Know-Who.

There was a waiter there who kept singing. He was dead funny. He held the tray on one hand and he sang I'm the King of the Swingers.

Chinese Toffee Apples are YUMMY too. I used my chopsticks. It was Pipsqueak. Mopsy can't use chopsticks. She had to have a spoon. Mum said she couldn't be doing with chopsticks. She had a fork. This is silly of her because chopsticks are Pipsqueak.

Mopsy was a pain. She goes, this has got mushrooms, this has got lumpy bits.

Dad made his chopsticks do a dance on the table. Mopsy thought it was funny. Everyone else was looking at us. It was INBARERSING.

POCKET MONEY DAY!

Only I spent 40p on an ice lolly.

This was not very smart.

Horace – 11 days

Running Away Money – £1.16p + £2 – 40p = £2.76

2 Double Deckers

1 Nutella sandwich

1 Snickers bar

Half a packet of chicken tikka crisps (they are not very nice)

SUNDAY

When Kelly goes to
Disneyland she will have
to speak French. She said,
oh no I won't but she will.
I am not going to tell her
about POMFREET, so she will
ask them for chips and
they won't know what she
is on about.

Mrs Fritwell came
round. She is all skinny
and her bracelets clank.
She said she was doing
a Bring-and-Buy for

Children's Cruelty in July
and would Mum do a
stall.

Mum said she thought
she'd have her hands full.

Mrs Fritwell said, surely
she'd be organised by July.

Mum said she was sorry
but she'd rather not commit
herself.

Mrs Fritwell desided —
oops — decided to have a go
at me. She said, well, Polly,
are you looking forward to
your New Baby?

I said, No I'm Not.

Mrs Fritwell said, oh
dear, that isn't very kind
of you, is it?

I said, I'm going through
a STROPPY FAZE.

She looked at
Mum like I wasn't
there and said her Laura
was a bit like that when
her Sophie was on the way
but as soon as Baby came
along Laura was a Little
Angel and used to fetch the
nappies.

I was going to say, I'm
not fetching nappies. But
Mum started moving Mrs
Fritwell to the door and
saying, so sorry, so kind

of you to think of me
and we'd try to come
to the Bring-and-Buy
anyway.

I said we'll BRING
the baby and
hope someone
BUYS it.

BABIES
F O R
S A L E

Mum said, that's quite enough from you, Madam! I don't know what Mrs Fritwell said, as she whispered it to Mum when she was out the door.

I asked Dad to write down POMFREET for me. He said, why do you want me to do that? I said, it's because I want to remember that I'm not going to tell Kelly what it is.

Dad said, I don't quite follow you, my darling, but I'll write it down for you.

Here is the bit of paper he wrote it on.

POMMES FRITES

It is still actually

POMFREET and Kelly will

not know how to say it.

I ate a Double Decker

Horace – 12 days

£2.76

1 Double Decker

1 Nutella sandwich

1 Snickers bar

I did actually eat the chicken tikka crisps. There didn't seem much point in only half a packet.

Snickers bars are very nice even though they have nuts. I am not ALLERGIC to nuts, I just don't like them. Not as much as I don't like BROCERLY.

I said to Mum, if Horace dies can we get a cat and she said, oh Polly, that doesn't sound very

kind to poor Horace. And
I said, yes but can we. She
said, no dear, she didn't
think so because cats are
a nuisance when you go
on holiday. I said, but
according to Dad we aren't
having a holiday anyway.
I said it in a SARCASTIC
voice but it was a complete
waste of being SARCASTIC
because she just said, yes
but they're a NUISANCE
anyway and could I be an
angel and fetch the scissors
from the kitchen drawer.

MONDAY

We had Diaries. I wrote about Dad and the chopsticks. Miss Price said, that isn't very nice when poor Daddy is trying to be nice to you, and anyway it is spelt EMBARRASSING. I don't think People should be embarrassing, SPECIALLY parents.

We did Queen Elizabeth in the Tudors. Queen Elizabeth was very grand. She liked to dance. She had lots of palaces. When she was old she wore a red wig.

I said, did she throw her poo out of the window too?

Miss Price said, probably it was only the poor people who did that, the rich people had someone to do it for them, and could we please talk about something else.

Alex is silly. She says when she is grown up she will be a pop star. You mustn't say Fluffy to her because Fluffy was her rabbit that died. Every time you say Fluffy she cries. But I think she is just doing it to get noticed. I don't think she is really crying.

Also she says her mum lets her watch television all day which is silly because nobody does.

I liked Kelly better when she was being my best friend.

She is still going to
Disneyland. She said she
might send me a postcard.

TUESDAY
Mrs Muldoon was in one
of her moods. She told us
all off this morning for:

1) running up the stairs.

2) being rude to the
dinner ladies (this is not
fair. It was only Darren
who was rude to the
dinner ladies. He said that
the chicken pie was really
dead mouse pie. The rest

of us are NEVER rude to the dinner ladies even though they are sometimes quite rude to us).

3) not playing proper games in the playground. She said all we do is HANG AROUND and we should learn to skip like she did when she was a little girl.

a b c d e f g h

Yes, and I bet they used
to throw their poo out of
the windows too when she
was a little girl.

Katy Poole's mum is a
friend of Mrs Muldoon.
She says that Mrs
Muldoon's son Paul plays
computer games all day and
will not make his bed. Mrs
Muldoon gets very cross
with him which is why she
takes it out on us.

Miss Price is not going
to marry Nigel. He is not
her best friend any more.
She says, can we just shut
up about it, please. I
suppose it is Embarrassing
her. But WE have to talk
about Embarrassing
things, so why not her?

I said to Lee — not
Center Parcs Lee who was
a girl but my class Lee
who is a boy — I said, why
is Six afraid of Seven?
Because Seven Eight Nine.
I said, do you get it, and
he said yes.

Then I heard him telling
Charlie the joke. He goes,

why is Eight afraid of
Nine? Because Eight Nine
Ten.

Really really STUPID.

WEDNESDAY

Darren said Horace had
probably been eaten by a
fox because they had a fox
in their street and it ate
everyone's rabbits. Alex
cried because he said
rabbits. He didn't even say
Fluffy. This is getting
really stupid.

I don't think Horace has
been eaten by a fox.

Today we did

Shakespeare. Shakespeare
ran away from home too!
Only he did it when he
was grown up. He ran all
the way to London and
wrote plays and became
famous. I think I'd like to
do that too. I don't know
how to get to London but
when I went with Granny
that time, we went on two
buses.

51

We did Silent Letters in spelling. KNOW KNIFE KNACK. I think they are silly. I said, why did we have to have Silent Letters and Miss Price said, I don't know, dear, I didn't invent the Rules. I said, suppose everyone said one day let's not have any more Silent Letters — then they wouldn't have to have them and we wouldn't have to do them. Miss Price said it didn't work that way. But if you are a Grown-Up why can't you just say no Silent Letters. Nobody likes them. They are really dumb.

Dumb has a silent letter
too. Dumb, Thumb.
Darren said Dumb,
Thumb, Bum, and Miss P
said, No dear, not Bum,
and can we not be rude all
the time.

Also: Big Elephants
Can't Always Use Small
Entrances.

Pink Elephants On Pills
Laugh Easily.

ANNOYING THINGS
ABOUT KELLY:

   1. She is going on and
on about Disneyland.

   2. She is not my best
friend.

   3. X Factor is her best
programme.

   4. Her new haircut is too
short at the back. It makes
her ears look all big.
She has very big ears
anyway.

Shakespeare died on his
birthday. That is so sad.

Dad said, perhaps we
could advertise in the
paper shop about Horace.
Has Anyone Seen Our
Hamster? Lots of people
advertise in the paper
shop.

One said, WANTED:

57

child's bicycle, any
condition. Dad said, I bet
that poor child doesn't
want their bicycle in any
condition.

I could advertise for a
family. WANTED: proper
family for nice girl in any
condition.

WHAT MY NEW FAMILY WILL BE LIKE:

They will live in a big house with a big garden in the country by the seaside. Near Center Parcs would be nice.

I will have lots of dogs — spaniels — and two ponies.

My ponies will be called Brandy and Danielle.

I WON'T HAVE SISTERS!!! OR BABIES!!!

My dad will not be ~~INBARASING~~ EMBARRASSING.

My mum will have an interesting job in a toy shop or a sweet shop.

59

She will not make
BROCERLY.

I will change my name to

Shanella

THURSDAY
Last night they were
moving about and
whispering. Dad came in
and said, are you asleep,
Poll? I pretended to be and
he said, it's all right, she's
dead to the world.

In the morning, Granny
was there. I said, where's
Mum?

She said, Mummy's gone
to the hospital.

I said, is it the baby?
and she said, yes, dear, I
think so.

I said, is having a baby
like an operation, only
on TV I saw this
rabbit having an operation.
She said, well it is and it
isn't. I said, does it hurt?
She said, well it does and
it doesn't.

Very helpful.

She said, look, hasn't
your mummy told you
all about these things
and maybe you should
ask her.

I said, how can I ask
her, she's in the hospital.

Granny said, how
about if we didn't go to
school today?

I said, what about the
Tudors?

Granny said she thought
one day didn't matter and
we could make some
cakes.

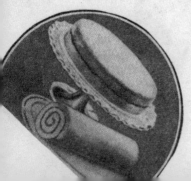

64

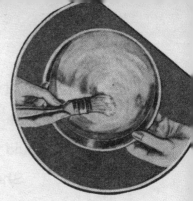

I said, the chocolate
ones with Rice Krispies,
and she said, oh no, that's
far too easy, I'll show you
how to make real cakes.
Grannies are peculiar.

I said I heard a scratchy
noise in the bathroom and
could it be Horace?

She said I must be
imagining things.

They always say that.

I expect Granny would
give me some money for
Running Away as long as
I didn't tell her what it
was for.

We watched Waybuloo.
We made cakes. Mopsy
said they had lumpy bits
and wouldn't eat them.
Granny said, all the more
for us. I like the ones with
Rice Krispies better but I

didn't say as I am much more politer than Mopsy.

Dad phoned from the hospital. He said everything was going well and give a big hug to his two Princesses.

This is quite boring really. I wish I was at school.

My Nutella sandwich has gone blue. I had to throw it away.

We had just put on the cartoons when the phone rang again. Granny went to pick it up.

She was going: Oooh! Oooh! Oooh! Wonderful.

She said, I must tell the girls.

She said, you have a little baby brother!

Mopsy said YIPPEE YIPPEE!

I said, did Dad know?

She said, that was Daddy on the phone, silly.

I said, when did we have to see the baby?

She said she wasn't sure but maybe in a day or two

and what did we want for
supper?

I said, could we have
Take-Away Pizza.

Mopsy said, I don't like
Pizza.

Granny said, maybe they
could make you a special
one.

I said, yes, with no
tomatoes, mushrooms or
cheese.

Granny said she and I
would have Pizza and she
would do Fish Fingers for
Mopsy.

I said to Granny, do
sandwiches go blue always?

She said, what a funny
question. Yes, I suppose so
in the end.

I said, do biscuits go
blue?

She said, I've never seen
a blue biscuit, come to
think of it.

I shall have to save
biscuits. I don't like
biscuits very much unless
they've got chocolate and
all our biscuits haven't got
chocolate in.

Chocolate Chip
Cookies!!! Yum yum
bubble gum. Cookies is

American for biscuits.
Americans eat peanut
butter and jelly sandwiches,
only it's actually jam.
They sound disgusting.

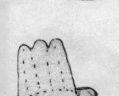

FRIDAY
Mum is coming home
tomorrow with It.

I wrote about the new
baby in Diary. Miss Price
made everybody clap. This
was silly as they don't

72

know what it is like
having a new baby.

Darren said his mum
had a new baby and it
sicked up everywhere.

Granny made peanut
butter and jelly — meaning
jam — sandwiches. They were
really yummy! Granny
tried one too and said they
were YUMMY. She said she
had never ever ever had
them before in her life and
if it hadn't been for me
she would never have tried
them.

Mopsy wouldn't eat
them because of the lumpy
bits.

I am sure it is Horace
behind the bath.

Granny gave me £5!!!

SATURDAY
It's here. It doesn't look
anything like a baby. It is
very small and has a red
face. I said mum should
take it back and get a
proper baby.

74

Mopsy is being really
silly. She is crying and
sucking her thumb.
Granny says there there
and cuddles her. Granny
says she is a bit jealous of
the new baby.

Why?

Dad said, we can't
decide what to call him.
Have you two got any
ideas?

Mopsy said, Iggle
Piggle.

I said, you can't call
him Iggle Piggle, stupid.

Mopsy said, why not?

I said because Iggle

Piggle isn't a proper
name.

She said, yes it is, it's
Iggle Piggle's proper
name.

Dad said, have you got
any better suggestions?

I said — I just thought of
it — what about William,
like William Shakespeare
because he ran away from
home and became famous.

I didn't mean to say
about running away from
home. It just came out.

Mum said, mmm
William. I like that.

Dad said, it has a good
ring to it.

She said, do you look
like a William, my poppet?
I said of course he
doesn't look like a
William, he looks like a
tomato.
Mum said, shall we

call you William, my little
tomato?

 She goes like that when she's
talking to him.

 Maybe William Shakespeare
looked like a tomato once.

It is really gross when she
feeds him. I said, well I NEVER did
that. She said, oh yes you did,
my darling.

 She is LYING. I never did THAT.

Running Away Fund — £7.76!

2 Double Deckers

1 Packet of salt and vinegar crisps

2 Home-made cakes

2 Biscuits

I will give the Snickers bar to Kelly as I really do not like nuts.

MONDAY

Kelly is being stupid. She says she has another secret only she can't tell me yet and this time it's a really good secret and I will like it.

I DON'T CARE ABOUT HER SECRET. IT IS DUMB.

William has these tiny little hands. The nails look

frilly. Mum said, put your finger
in his hand, and I did and he
held it all tightly! Mum says he
knows you're his big sister.

I don't think he does yet.

Mum said it was very nice for
him to have a big sister. She was
very glad I was his sister. She
said I deserved a present for
being a nice sister.
I haven't decided if I am going
to be a nice sister yet. Maybe I
will be if William is a nice baby.
It is all down to him.

Granny is going to make my
lunch for the school trip. She
said, what do you like and I
said, I don't mind.

She said, I'm glad to hear it

because your mummy was an awful fusspot when it came to packed lunches and everything else. I said, did she like BROCERLY, and Granny said, no, probably not. She hated everything green. She hated peas and salad and beans and carrots. Carrots aren't green but she hated them too.

I said, did she hate lumpy bits? Granny said, I expect so. She wouldn't eat her packed lunch one day because Granny had put special chicken bits in and Mum wouldn't eat it because nobody else had chicken bits and she wanted Marmite sandwiches.

I said I'd eat chicken bits, and Granny said, good, but she

didn't actually have any so would peanut butter and jam do and I said yummy.

TUESDAY

Today we went to the Tower of London. Darren and Luke were messing about in the coach and Miss Price had to tell them to shut up.

Our Beefeater was called Kevin. They are called Beefeaters because they used to eat lots of beef but they don't have to any more. They are really called The Yeomen of the Guard. Kevin was quite nice but he

told all these horrible
stories about how people
had their heads chopped
off. Everybody could have
their heads chopped off in
those days if they upset
Queen Elizabeth. They
came up the river and
through a gate called
Traitor's Gate. There was
a tower called The Bloody
Tower.

Sometimes it took lots of goes to cut someone's head off as the axe wasn't very sharp. People used to stand around and watch.

All the boys thought it was very funny, but I didn't.

Anyway, I think Kevin was making the stories horrible just for the boys.

Alex pretended to cry

when we saw the place
where they had their heads
chopped off. So of course
we all had to notice her.

The ravens are huge! If
they run away, the Tower
will fall down. It is just as
well that it is ravens and
not hamsters.

We saw armour which
was boring and the crown
jewels. We had to wait in
a long long line and then
we had to go by very fast.

They were nice but they would be very heavy to wear. Darren said he would steal the big diamond and I said they would chop his head off if he did. He said he would get his dad to see to them. I said don't be silly.

Of course, Darren and Luke were nearly late for the coach going back and Miss Price was cross. Then on the way back he kept pretending to chop everyone's heads off with his lunch box. Miss Price said, that's enough Darren and he tried to chop her head off. She got really cross then.

Kelly and I sat next to each other on the coach back. She said Lisa wasn't really her sister. But she still wouldn't tell me the secret.

WEDNESDAY
When we finish the Tudors we will do the Greeks.

A B C D E F G H I

We have twenty
spellings to learn by
Friday!!! I can do most of
them but not all of them.

SOLDIER

ENGLAND

$\times 8 = 8$ PRETTY·

$\times 8 = 16$

$\times 8$ Could is popsy — I could

$\times 8 = 24$ spell that when I was one,

$\times 8 = 32$ I bet.

$\times 8 = 40$ We are on the eight

$\times 8 = 48$ times table. That is a

$\times 8 = 56$ really hard one.

$\times 8 = 64$

$\times 9 = ?$ There are painters in the

$\times 8 = 80$ school and everything

$\times 8 = 88$ stinks. Mrs Muldoon says

$\times 8 = 96$ we have to be very careful

not to bump into them. I

think it is their job to be

very careful, not ours.

Darren says all babies do that thing with holding your hand.

Kelly is still going on and on.

I am sure Horace is behind the bath.

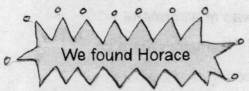

We found Horace

Dad came up and I told him about the noises. He got his screwdriver thing and took a bit of the bath off. Horace was there kind of all scrunched up. Dad

said there was a damp bit
so he had water. He looks
a bit scruffy. We put him
in his cage and gave him
water and food. He just
sat there. I don't think he
was at all grateful.

Hamsters are a bit
boring. A cat would be
nicer.

Alex dresses her cat up
and puts him in a pram.
She says he likes it. If I
were a cat, I would not like
being put in a pram by
Alex. If we had a cat, I
would treat it better.

Horace is cute, though.
I'm glad he's back.

I had to throw the cakes away. They had gone all horrible. It is very difficult to keep food for running away. I wonder what Shakespeare did. They didn't have Double Deckers in his day so it must have been hard.

THURSDAY
Kelly said, have they told you yet and I said, told me what and she said, never mind.

I think one of the painters fancies Miss Price. He is the good looking one. The others are ugly.

He winks at her and says
Hello, Miss, when she goes
past. She looks all huffy.

But I bet he is better
looking than Nigel. She
might as well let him be
her boyfriend. I shall tell
her this tomorrow.

The phone just went.
Mum took it in the hall
and then came and
beckoned to Dad and he
went out and they were
talking. When they came
in, they were all
giggly. I think they
have a secret.
All these secrets
are very irritating.

FRIDAY
I KNOW WHAT THE
SECRET IS!

It was Kelly's mum on
the phone! They want to
take me to Disneyland
with them!

Mum and Dad said they
were talking about it, and
I can go!

It is quite soon. We will
go on the train and stay in
a special hotel. Granny
will help them out and
give me some money to
spend. I told them I
already have £7.76p saved,
though I did not say what
for.

Kelly said she was not
allowed to tell me until
they had told Mum and
Dad.

I told her about
POMFREET and I told her
about GLAS. She was very
glad I did. We will have
lots of POMFREET and GLAS
when we are in France.
Kelly is much nicer now. It
will be great.

95

I won't be able to run away for a bit, though I am still going to. Probably I'll wait till I'm grown up like Shakespeare.

Maybe when I come back from Disneyland, William will look like a proper baby.